To Jack —

My beloved hope

Prince — I hope

you have a World

of adventures.

love.

Mimi

Princess Aisha
and the Cave of Judgment

Kay Lovelace Taylor

Illustrated by

Karen C. Rhine

© Text Copyright
Kay Lovelace Taylor

© Illustration Copyright
Karen C. Rhine

KLT & Associates
E-mail : lovelacetaylor@aol.com
Telephone : 480-342-9638
Fax: 480-342-9639

Order Online:
www.KayLovelaceTaylor.com

First Addition, Second Printing.

ISBN-13 978-0-9799119-0-3

Library of Congress Catalog Card
Number

2007934860

Printed by Bookmasters, Inc.
Ashland, Ohio, United States
Book Sales

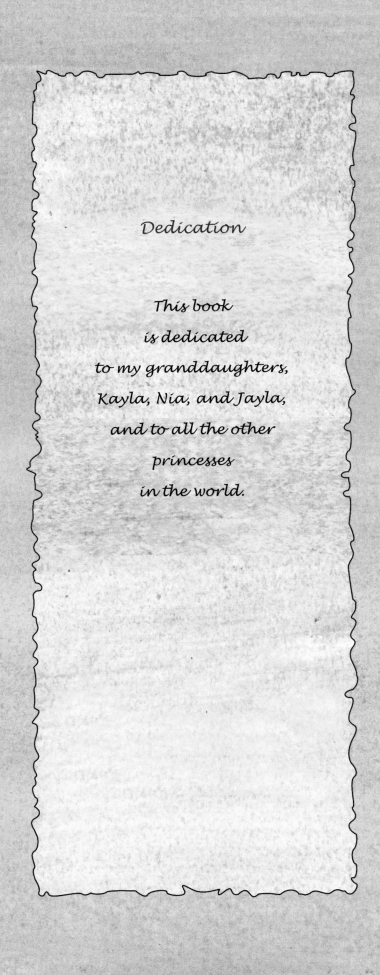

Dedication

This book
is dedicated
to my granddaughters,
Kayla, Nia, and Jayla,
and to all the other
princesses
in the world.

Once upon a time, far away, there lived a king who ruled over the ancient kingdom of Kush in Africa. King Piye and his wife, Queen Abar, lived in a magnificent palace in the capital city of Napata and ruled over a vast land as far as the eye could see.

The king and queen had a very beautiful and inquisitive daughter named Aisha who spent more time daydreaming than paying attention to her studies. Aisha spent hours making up adventures that she, and her beautiful chestnut stallion Thaoma, would triumph over.

A real adventure for Princess Aisha was traveling every morning with her father, King Piye, to the edge of the palace grounds. Once there, the king would listen as the people gave him the daily report on how his kingdom was doing. King Piye wanted to know if the kingdom was safe for all, but particularly for his daughter Princess Aisha. He would inquire about the weather to make certain it posed no threat and that there were enough food and water to feed every living creature, both big and small, that occupied the kingdom.

One morning when the King asked for the report, he learned there was a very strange sound coming from the northeast part of the kingdom. The king asked what the noise sounded like, and one of the people reporting said, "It sounds like someone moaning."

"Moaning?" said the King.

"Yes, moaning, your Highness."

"Why would there be moaning in our kingdom when we wish nothing but happiness for all who live here?"

For the kingdom was very beautiful. Every day there were bright clear skies, beautiful palm trees that swayed in the wind, majestic mountains in the distance, and a magnificent river full of fish that flowed into the deep blue sea. There were also tropical flowers of every color in the rainbow. And yes, there were many rainbows.

After hearing the report, King Piye immediately summoned ten of his strongest riders, five men and five women, to go to the northeast side of the kingdom to see if they could find where the strange noise was coming from.

Princess Aisha begged to go with the riders but King Piye would not permit it because there could be danger.

The riders rode all day and most of the night to get to the northeast region of the kingdom and when they did, they heard a strange sound, almost like a wind whistling through the trees.

As they rode closer, the riders could tell that what they were hearing was the sad and pain-filled voice of a human coming from a cave inside one of the mountains.

The riders called out, "Who's in there?"

No one answered.

One of the riders called out again but this time louder, "Is anyone there?" And just as they were about to give up, a very weak voice called back.

"Yes, I am lost and injured."

"What is your name, and where do you come from?"

"My name is Magasa, and I come from a land east of Napata, called Gebel Barkal."

"Come out so we can see you."

"I cannot come out; my injuries will not allow me to walk."

"Have no fear," said the riders, "We will come in and get you."

But when they entered the cave, instead of finding a person, they found a hideous monster so appalling that they turned around quickly without saying a word and ran out of the cave.

Once outside, they questioned each other and asked, "Did you see what I saw?"

Each confirmed that they saw a huge monster with an abnormal shape. They all agreed that they must protect the kingdom, so they sealed the mouth of the cave with enormous boulders and rode as fast as they could to report to the king the danger they had come upon.

Princess Aisha was playing in the royal chamber, pretending to be on safari. She imagined she was surrounded by lions and was skillfully opposing their charges when she heard the riders enter.

Her mother and father were visiting with dignitaries in another part of the palace and had appointed the Viceroy of Affairs to hear all reports.

Princess Aisha was supposed to be with the royal tutor. She quickly hid herself so as not to be seen just as the Viceroy of Affairs sat down in the adjoining reception room to hear the riders' report.

Princess Aisha listened without making a sound as the riders explained that an injured monster had found its way to the kingdom. They shared that although they did not get a good look at him, they saw his shadow on the wall of the cave, and he was huge, deformed, and hideous.

Princess Aisha gasped as the riders told the Viceroy of Affairs that the kingdom need not fear because the riders had sealed off the cave with boulders, leaving the monster to die from his wounds.

She waited for the Viceroy to ask how the riders knew the monster was dangerous, or to ask, "Could it be a good and kind monster just in need of some help?" But instead, the Viceroy congratulated the riders and rewarded them for protecting the kingdom from such a dangerous creature.

Princess Aisha could not sleep that night. All she could think about was how often her parents told her to never judge another person based on looks or what others have to say.

She tossed and turned until she finally sat straight up in her bed. She knew what she must do.

The next morning, she told her father and mother that she had been invited to visit her friends for a few days, and with their permission, she mounted her horse and rode off to the north.

Before doing so, she stopped off to see her best friend(s), (Insert your child(ren)'s name) and said she was on a secret mission and that no one must know where she was going.

Aisha made (insert your child(ren)'s name) promise not to tell. With that promise, Princess Aisha rode off towards the mountains in search of the cave the riders had sealed off.

Although very young, Aisha was an excellent rider and she soon found the tracks left by the riders around one of the caves. She dismounted and moved closer to the mouth of the cave.

Aisha saw small openings, leaned closely, and called out, "Is anyone in there?"

Someone called out, "Hello, hello, please help me."

"What's your name?" Aisha called back.

"My name is Magasa, and I am injured. Can you help me?"

"Why should I help you?" I understand you have come to do harm to my people. You are an evil monster who might do harm to me."

"No, no," cried Magasa. "Who told you that? I am lost and injured badly; please help me."

Aisha listened to the voice and although it was very weak, the voice also sounded very kind. So Aisha thought and thought. What should she do? "I know," thought Aisha, "My father said you can always tell a good person by what he values most."

"Magasa, I will help you, but I am alone and the boulders are very big. What if I cannot move the boulders and you die?"

"Fear not kind child for I know you have done your best and that is all I ask of you. Except, if you cannot move the boulders, will you grant me one last request? Please send word to my mother and father, who live in Gerbel Barkal, that I fell from my horse, and through no fault of anyone, I could not recover."

Aisha was touched deeply by Magasa's concern for his parents and knew that he was not a dangerous monster. This was a kind person. An evil person would blame everyone for his troubles and would not think of anyone's feelings but his own.

How could Princess Aisha free Magasa?

Suddenly she remembered seeing one of the palace guards move a very big stone by pulling it with a rope tied to a horse. She called Thaoma and removed a lasso from the side of her saddle. Aisha tightened the lasso around one of the boulders, tied the other end to her saddle, and then led Thaoma away from the boulder. As the horse moved, the rope tightened and the boulder began to move, just a little at first.

When the boulder moved, it jolted another boulder, then another, and another, until finally all of the boulders fell, creating a small avalanche that uncovered the mouth of the cave.

Aisha heard Magasa moan, and she called out to him, "Are you all right?" But he did not say anything. She was so frightened. All she could remember is what the riders said: "a huge, hideous monster."

But she knew she had to go inside the cave. Aisha called out to Magasa again, and as she did, she saw a shadow on the wall of the cave move.

It was huge, without much of a shape, but obviously the disfigured shadow of Magasa.

As Aisha got closer, something was very strange. She could see the back of Magasa's head, and as she approached him, what appeared to be his body in the shadow were actually three boulders he was lying behind. His legs were extended making it appear in the shadow that he had three legs.

Magasa was not a monster at all; he was a very handsome young man who weakly smiled at her as he told her what happened to him and how he crawled into the cave.

Magasa shared how he was riding to the city of Napata to speak with King Piye about helping his people who had suffered from a tremendous typhoon that ripped through their city, destroyed their crops, and killed many of their people.

While he was riding, his horse was startled and threw him on the rocks in front of the cave. His horse ran away, and he was left all alone and in great pain from his fall. Not knowing what he might encounter, he dragged himself into the cave, hoping to keep safe and warm until he was strong enough to venture out and find his way.

Magasa said riders had come and he thought surely they were going to help him. To his amazement, however, they quickly left without a word and sealed off the cave. He called out to the riders over and over again, but they did not respond.

Aisha looked into Magasa's eyes and said, "Fear not kind sir; I am Aisha, daughter of King Piye, and you will be safe and well again very soon. The prince could not believe his good fate. Aisha helped Magasa on her horse, and they rode back to her father's kingdom.

When Aisha and Magasa approached the palace, there were Magasa's mother and father who had traveled to Napata to find their missing son. Everyone rejoiced when Aisha and Magasa arrived. King Piye praised his daughter for listening to her conscience and not judging a person falsely.

As for the riders, they apologized and volunteered to accompany Magasa and his parents back to Gebel Barkal to help rebuild their city with the generous materials and supplies given by King Piye and Queen Abar.

Aisha and her family want everyone to know you should never judge a person by looks alone or by what others say; always find out for yourself.

The End.